LONGBEARD
THE WIZARD

LONGBEARD THE WIZARD

by SID FLEISCHMAN

Illustrated by CHARLES BRAGG

An Atlantic Monthly Press Book

Little, Brown and Company
Boston   Toronto

Books by Sid Fleischman

MR. MYSTERIOUS & COMPANY

BY THE GREAT HORN SPOON!

THE GHOST IN THE NOONDAY SUN

CHANCY AND THE GRAND RASCAL

LONGBEARD THE WIZARD

For Emilie

Once upon a time there was a king. And once upon a time there was another king.

King Barbos the Old was very rich. He was forever scheming of ways to grow richer. To delight his eye he lined his vast treasure rooms with mirrors. His chests of jewels and gold doubled and tripled and mutiplied beyond counting. But still he was not satisfied.

Not far away lived King Sandor the Young. He ruled over a small, barren kingdom with a simple village standing inside an ancient stone wall. Here crows, as tame as pigeons, flocked about the square and ate out of children's hands.

King Sandor's palace was small, with only one treasure room heavily laced with cobwebs and containing a mere handful of copper coins.

His people had holes in their boots and some had no boots at all. Still they sang and danced like gypsies and cheered each other with funny stories. Poets wrote verses about the crows. Minstrels strummed their lutes and the fruit vendor could juggle five ripe pears—if he had five ripe pears.

Watching from his window, the young monarch often thought that everyone was doing things more amusing than ruling a poor kingdom. He felt useless and unhappy. He wished that he were not king at all.

Then he remembered a box of magic tricks among his old toys. He began to practice and soon he could catch copper coins out of the air.

He would not be king. He would be a magician.

So one market day he put on a false black beard, a magician's robe and a tall hat decorated with moons and stars.

He slipped out of the palace and beat a drum to gather a crowd. "I am Longbeard the Wizard!" he announced, and plucked coppers from ladies' ears and men's beards and children's noses.

Everyone gasped with delight. No one recognized him. The long beard made him seem older and the tall hat made him seem taller.

But visiting that day were three huge men in the service
of King Barbos. They gazed in amazement. They mistook
the coppers, glistening in the setting sun, for gold coins.

They whispered among themselves. Here was a rare prize for King Barbos! They would follow the wizard and kidnap him and deliver him to the old King, who would reward them handsomely.

They mounted their horses and followed Longbeard
through the crowd.

In the dark shadows of a stone arch they pounced upon the wizard, put him in a sack and dashed away through the gate and out of the kingdom.

When the young sorcerer was pulled out of the sack he found himself in the palace of King Barbos the Old. Guards marched him along gloomy halls and up winding stone steps to a narrow door. The old King, with great gobs of cotton in his ears, stuck his head out of the door and peered at the visitor. He smelled of brimstone and cloves and acid. With strange machines and strange chemicals, he was trying to discover the secret of turning lead into gold. He was angry at being disturbed.

"Take him to the Queen," he growled, and banged the door shut.

So Longbeard the Wizard was marched back down the winding stone steps and along the gloomy halls to the Queen.

Queen Gibble-Gabble, as everyone called her, was the despair of the kingdom. She talked from morning till night. She gossiped and chattered and gibble-gabbled. She talked to herself. She talked while she ate. She even talked in her sleep. That was why the King wore cotton in his ears.

"Wizard!" she commanded. "Pluck! Plick! Pluck! I shall have new gowns and larger jewels and a greater crown! Plick

my arms full! Pluck my chamber full! Pluck, plick, pluck, and I will be so beautiful that every queen will be jealous of me!"

"Certainly not," replied Longbeard the Wizard, adjusting his false whiskers. "Absolutely not."

So he was thrown into the dungeon and fed on wormy black bread and water until he should change his mind.

All night long the Queen's voice echoed along the halls and seeped into the dungeon. She chattered about gowns of peacock feathers and slippers carved from emeralds and pearls the size of eggs to dangle from her neck. "Queen Gibble-Gabble is talking in her sleep again," the guard sighed.

Longbeard wondered what a *real* wizard would do. Just before dawn he found the answer and asked to be taken before the King.

The King had hardly slept a wink all night—even with cotton in his ears. The marble walls of his chamber still echoed with the Queen's chittering and chattering.

Again he scowled at the young prisoner brought before him. "What do you want?" he roared.

"I am Longbeard the Wizard," announced King Sandor.

"What, what, what?" said the old King, pulling the wads of cotton from his ears. "Speak up! Speak up!"

"*I am Longbeard the Wizard!*" the young King repeated. "I will magic the Queen out of gibbering and jabbering and gibbling and gabbling. She will be as silent as a mouse."

"Impossible!" King Barbos groaned.

"Nothing is impossible to Longbeard the Wizard!" said King Sandor. "You must pay me one hundred gold pieces and free me forever from the dungeon."

The old King thought it over. "Agreed," he said finally. "All my wise men have failed. If you fail I shall feed you into my machine and turn you into a lump of gold—as soon as I get the machine working right."

"Agreed," said the wizard. King Barbos sent for one hundred gold pieces, which the young King hid in the secret pockets of his magician's robe.

Queen Gibble-Gabble was chattering away when he was
escorted to her chamber. She was having breakfast in bed—
an omelet of butterfly eggs stuffed with tongues of hum-
mingbirds.

"Ah, you have changed your mind!" she smiled victoriously.

"Yes," said the wizard. "I will pluck coins from the air as long as you keep talking. The moment you stop, I will stop."

"Splendid!" she laughed, and began to gibber and jabber. "Pluck! Plick! Pluck!"

Longbeard dipped into his secret pockets and soon was plucking coins from candlesticks and motes of sunlight and flowers in their vases. The Queen gibbled and gabbled. Then he tweaked her red nose and a stream of gold pieces clinked out.

The magician had almost used up the hundred gold coins when Queen Gibble-Gabble thought to ask *why* she must keep talking.

"It is a secret every magician, wizard and sorcerer knows," replied Longbeard.

"A secret? What secret?"

"I cannot reveal it."

"I command you!" said the Queen.

Longbeard the Wizard bowed low, being careful not to let his hat slip off. "My Lady, I have been buying your words with these coins."

"Nonsense!"

"It is revealed in books of black magic that each of us is born to speak a certain number of words. Just so many—and not a word more. When we use up our supply we die *at once*."

Queen Gibble-Gabble turned white. She slapped a hand over her mouth and from that moment on refused to speak another word. It might be her very last.

Longbeard the Wizard smiled behind his whiskers. How foolish she was, he thought! By plucking a string of silly words from his sleeve he had magicked the Queen into silence.

For the first time in years King Barbos could walk through the palace without cotton in his ears. And he heard that the sorcerer with the long black beard could pluck gold pieces out of thin air.

He promptly poured out his strange chemicals, which didn't work, and kicked in his strange machines, which didn't work, and commanded the magician to fill his treasury to the roof.

"Certainly not," said Longbeard wearily. "Absolutely not."

"You'll change your mind in the dungeon!" said the old King.

"You promised to free me forever from the dungeon," Longbeard reminded him.

So the wizard was marched to the tower instead. He was locked in and given all the wormy black bread he cared to eat.

That night the unhappy prisoner sent a guard with a message to the Queen, who had gone to bed with a great wad of cotton in her mouth so that she wouldn't talk in her sleep.

The message, which he wrote out among the moons and stars of his hat, dipping his finger in dust, read:

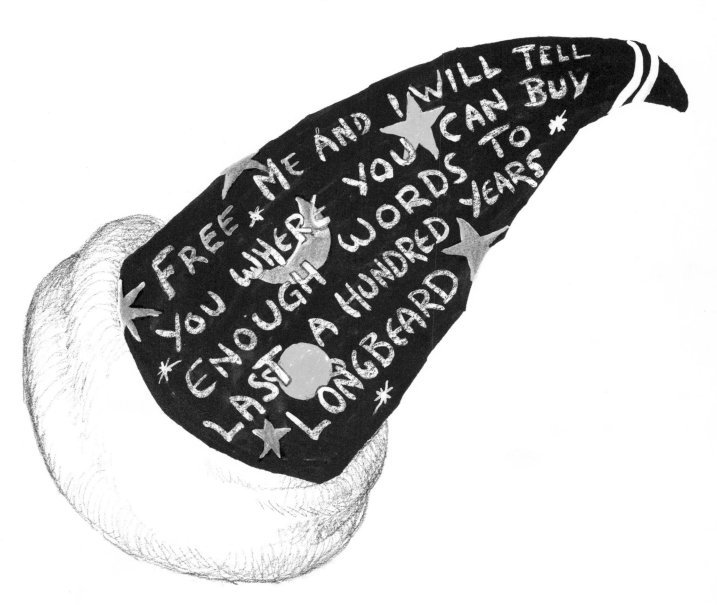

FREE ME AND I WILL TELL YOU WHERE YOU CAN BUY ENOUGH WORDS TO LAST A HUNDRED YEARS LONGBEARD

It was too tempting an offer for the Queen to refuse. She visited the wizard in the tower, returning his hat without uttering a word.

He told her that he must be put in a sack and returned to the neighboring kingdom. If she would visit there on market day, he would magic things so that she could gibble-gabble again to her heart's content.

The Queen nodded and snapped her fingers at the guard.
By morning Longbeard was back in his own kingdom.

He took off his long false beard and tall hat and magician's
robe. Then he called together his people and made plans for
market day.

Queen Gibble-Gabble arrived in her royal coach, scattering
the crows in the square. She was overjoyed at what she saw.
Signs everywhere said:

WORDS FOR SALE

She immediately went on a shopping spree. She bought
THEs and ANDs and BUTs—ten for a penny. She bought
YESes and NOs, which were sold in pairs like shoes. She
bought longer words, even though they were more expensive.

She bought hundreds of words, thousands of words, and sent the carriage back for more money. In her haste she even bought words she didn't understand, like ARROGANCE and CREDULOUS and VANITY and AVARICE and LOQUACIOUS.

By nightfall she was gone.

From his window King Sandor could see the joy among
his people. Their pockets jingled and jangled with coins—
enough to last a hundred years.

The fruit vendor ordered a pair of boots from the cobbler and the cobbler ordered a winter coat from the tailor. The poets wrote verses about Queen Gibble-Gabble, the minstrels sang songs about King Sandor, and they all ordered seven-course dinners at the inn.

Before long, rumors reached King Sandor's small kingdom that again the halls of King Barbos's palace echoed with
the Queen's chatter and gossip and gibble-gabble.

And again King Barbos the Old stuffed cotton in his ears.

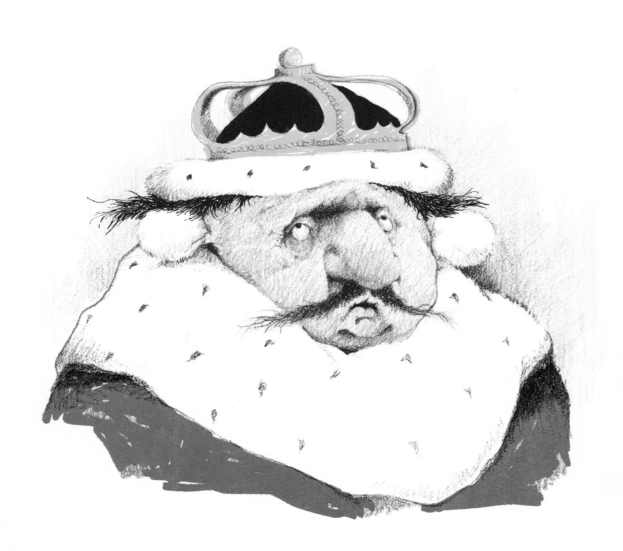

But King Sandor the Young had no time for rumors. Longbeard the Wizard was learning to pluck a flock of crows from a hat.